Last One in Is a Rotten Egg!

Last One in Is a Rotten Egg!

Diane deGroat

HARPERCOLLINS*PUBLISHERS*

Last One in Is a Rotten Egg!
Copyright © 2007 by Diane deGroat

Manufactured in China.
Library of Congress Cataloging-in-Publication Data is available.
ISBN-10: 0-06-089294-3 — ISBN-10: 0-06-089295-1 (lib. bdg.)
ISBN-13: 978-0-06-089294-4 — ISBN-13: 978-0-06-089295-1 (lib. bdg.)

Typography by Jeanne L. Hogle
1 2 3 4 5 6 7 8 9 10
❖
First Edition

Other Books About Gilbert

No More Pencils, No More Books, No More Teacher's Dirty Looks!
Brand-new Pencils, Brand-new Books
Liar, Liar, Pants on Fire
Good Night, Sleep Tight, Don't Let the Bedbugs Bite
We Gather Together—Now Please Get Lost!
Jingle Bells, Homework Smells
Happy Birthday to You, You Belong in a Zoo
Trick or Treat, Smell My Feet
Roses Are Pink, Your Feet Really Stink

G ilbert and Lola were excited—their cousin Wally was coming! They hadn't seen him in a long time, and they were looking forward to his visit.

"He's here!" Lola shouted from the window.

The door burst open and Wally tumbled in. "Last one
in is a rotten egg!" he yelled.

Uncle Gus appeared in the door behind him. "Hello,
all," he said, picking up the umbrella stand that Wally
had knocked over.

Wally was much bigger than Gilbert remembered. He
was almost as tall as Uncle Gus!

"You're just in time for lunch," Mother said. "I made soup and sandwiches."

"Last one in is a rotten egg!" Wally shouted, running to the table.

Gilbert walked quickly to his seat. Lola walked quickly too. They didn't want to be rotten eggs!

Mother didn't care if she was a rotten egg. She carefully
served the soup before sitting down. She said to Wally,
"You'll have fun this afternoon. There's an Easter egg hunt in
the park."

Wally made a face and said, "Egg hunts are for babies."

But Gilbert wanted his friends to meet Wally. "There's a prize if you find the most eggs," he said cheerfully.

"And there's a prize if you find the golden egg," Lola added. "I'm going to look real hard and find it."

"I'll go," said Wally. "But I still think it's stupid." Then he stuffed the last of his peanut butter sandwich into his mouth, saying, "Lath one finithed is a wotten egg!"

At the park, Wally didn't want to stay with Gilbert and his friends. He took a basket and headed for the starting line.

"Your cousin is not very friendly," Patti said.

"He just wants to win," Gilbert answered. Gilbert wanted to win too, so when the whistle blew, he ran after Wally, calling, "Last one up the hill is a rotten egg!"

They raced in all directions, looking under bushes and behind trees.

"I found one," Gilbert shouted from the bushes.

"I found two!" Wally yelled from behind a tree.

Patti and Lola searched the tall grass. "I can't find any eggs," Lola whined.

"Look," Patti said. "There's one right by your foot!"

"I found one!" Lola cried. She proudly put the green plastic egg into her basket.

Gilbert and Wally ran over to see if more eggs were hiding in the tall grass. Gilbert was anxious to find more because Wally's basket was almost full!

But Lola's basket was almost empty.

Gilbert sighed and gave Lola some eggs from his own basket. "Thanks!" she said. "Let's find more!" Together they ran toward a patch of trees.

Suddenly Lola stopped running and shouted, "I see it! I see the golden egg up in that tree!" She stood on her toes, but she couldn't reach it.

Neither could Gilbert. They needed someone tall. He called to Wally, "Lola found the golden egg, but we can't get it!"

Wally said, "No problem." He stood on his toes and stretched higher and higher.

"I got it!" he shouted.

"Yay, Wally!" Gilbert said.

Wally dropped the egg into his basket and walked off.

"Hey!" Gilbert called to Wally. "No fair! Lola found that egg!"

"But I'm the one who picked it up," Wally said.

Lola cried, "I'm telling!"

But Wally just said, "Tattletale!"

The whistle blew. The hunt was over, and everyone headed back to the starting line.

Wally had more eggs in his basket than anyone else. He also had the golden egg. Wally said, "I like egg hunts! Let's go see what the prizes are!"

Gilbert had an idea. "You're right," he said. "Let's go see." Then he shouted, "Last one down is a rotten egg!"

Wally took off and ran down the hill. "I win!" he said. When he looked back, Gilbert and Lola were still at the top, picking up all the eggs that had fallen out of Wally's basket—including the golden one!

"Oops . . . ," Wally said when he saw his empty basket.

For finding the golden egg, Lola won a beautiful sugar egg with a scene inside.

For finding the most eggs, Gilbert won an Easter basket filled with chocolate eggs, cream eggs, and his favorite—marshmallow eggs.

But Gilbert didn't feel right about taking the basket.
He walked over to Wally and said, "You really found the
most eggs, not me. You should have the prize."

Wally turned red. "Maybe we could share it?" he
suggested.

And they did!